SPORK

Written by **Kyo Maclear**

Illustrated by **Isabelle Arsenault**

KIDS CAN PRESS

Spork was neither
spoon nor **fork** …

fork

spoon

Spork

… but a bit of **both**.

He had a **mum** and a **dad** ...

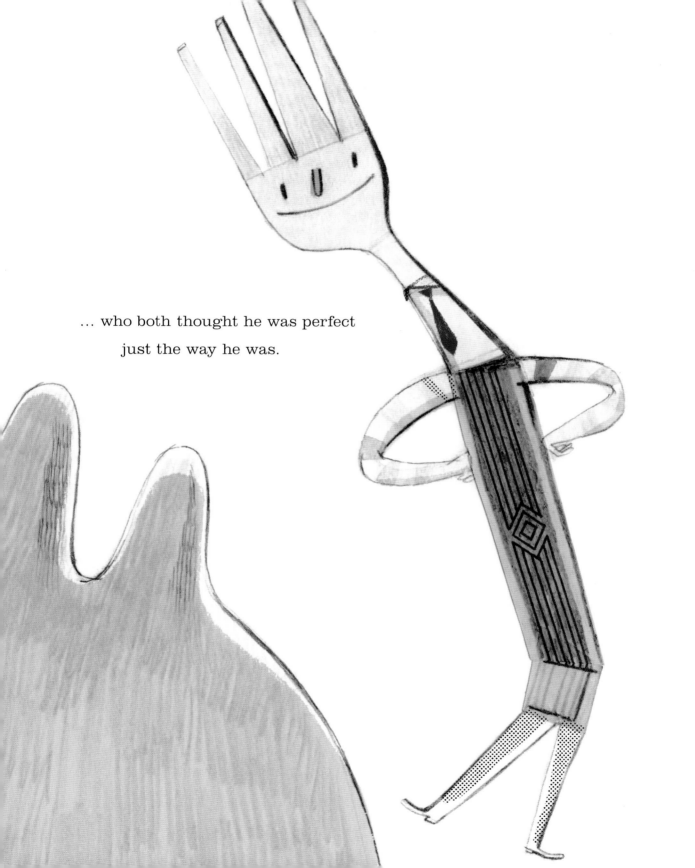

... who both thought he was perfect
just the way he was.

But **Spork** stuck out.

In his kitchen, forks were forks and
spoons were spoons. Cutlery customs were
followed closely. Mixing was uncommon.
Naturally, there were rule breakers: knives
who loved chopsticks, tongs who married forks.
But such families were unusual.

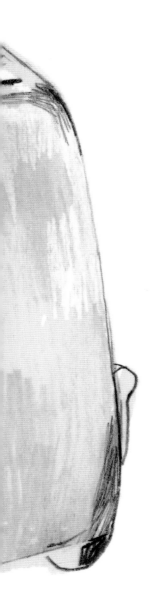

One day, after the billionth time he was asked "What are you, anyway?" and the zillionth time he was passed over when the table was being set ...

... Spork sighed and thought, "It must be easier to be a single thing." And he decided he'd try to pick just **ONE** thing to be.

He thought he should start by fixing

his head. He put on a bowler hat to look

more spoonish. But the forks

thought he was too round.

Then he made a paper crown to look
more forkish. But the spoons
thought he was too pointy.

Spork wondered if there were other lonely creatures out there with **no matching kind**, who never got chosen to be at the table.

At dinnertime, he watched from the drawer
while the spoons played pea hockey and skillfully balanced boiled
eggs. He sat off to the side while the forks raked fancy patterns in
the mashed potatoes and twirled noodles around in complicated
circles like rhythmic gymnasts. And at the end of this and every
other meal, Spork looked on while the
others enjoyed a super-bubbly
bath in the sink.

Until one morning, a **messy thing** arrived.
This messy thing had obviously never heard of cutlery
customs or table manners. No. This messy thing smeared and
spilled and flung and clumped and dripped without a care.

"Wait!" said the forks.

But the messy thing did not wait.

"Careful!"

said the spoons. But the messy
thing was not careful.

"Help!" said the forks
while the messy thing continued to
slop and splatter.

"Quick!"
said the spoons.

Now, a fork may be good for poking and picking.

And a spoon may be fine for scooping and stirring.

But this messy thing with its slurpy and clumpy half-finished food bits needed **something else**.
Something that could do all sorts of things at once.
Something flexible and easy to hold.

Something that was neither

spoon nor fork but a

bit of both.

That's when **Spork** landed.

The messy thing saw Spork and immediately

stopped. And gurgled.

It grabbed Spork and held him motionless in its fist.

It tapped him once and let out a cheerful **shriek**.

It wagged Spork excitedly up and down.

And that's how **Spork** finally and happily found his way to the table.

Just a bit round. Just a bit pointy.

Just right.

To Yoshi and Mika (my sons), David (cocreator),
Tara–Isabelle–Karen (dream team) and to all the
amazing sporks and misfits in my life — K.M.

To Arnaud and Florent, my two messy things,
and to Fred, who helps me handle their everyday
splashes! Love you all — I.A.

First paperback edition 2017

Text © 2010 Kyo Maclear
Illustrations © 2010 Isabelle Arsenault

Kids Can Press gratefully acknowledges the financial
support of the Government of Ontario, through the
Ontario Media Development Corporation; the Ontario
Arts Council; the Canada Council for the Arts; and
the Government of Canada, through the CBF, for our
publishing activity.

Published in Canada and the U.S. by Kids Can Press Ltd.
25 Dockside Drive, Toronto, ON M5A 0B5

Kids Can Press is a Corus Entertainment Inc. company

www.kidscanpress.com

The artwork in this book was rendered in mixed
media and assembled digitally.
The text is set in Clarendon Light.

Edited by Tara Walker
Designed by Karen Powers

Printed and bound in Tseung Kwan O, NT Hong Kong,
China, in 12/2018 by Paramount Printing Co. Ltd.

CM 10 0 9 8 7 6 5
CM PA 17 0 9 8 7 6 5 4 3

**Library and Archives Canada Cataloguing
in Publication**

Maclear, Kyo, 1970–, author
   Spork / written by Kyo Maclear ; illustrated
by Isabelle Arsenault. — First paperback edition 2017.

ISBN 978-1-55337-736-8 (bound)
ISBN 978-1-77138-805-4 (paperback)

I. Arsenault, Isabelle, 1978–, illustrator II. Title.

PS8625.L435S66 2017   jC813'.6
C2016-905174-9